KNOW GREATER LOVE

Joseph Nesi

ISBN 978-1-68526-565-6 (Paperback)
ISBN 978-1-68526-568-7 (Digital)

Covenant Books
11661 Hwy 707
Murrells Inlet, SC 29576
www.covenantbooks.com

To my beautiful wife, Linda, and my friends Debbie Parr and Tami Gibbons. If it were not for their constant love and wonderful listening skills, I may not have completed any of these stories. My wife led me along this journey of writing with all the skills that a teacher of her caliber has in her possession. I would also like to dedicate these stories to my children: my daughters Esther, Rebecca, Sarah, Jessica, and Mary, and my son, Joseph. It is my hope that you will someday share these stories with my grandchildren and the next generation of my much-loved family.

THE MEANING BEHIND
BIBLICAL NAMES

Why I Chose Them

Jacob: May God protect
Anna: Gracious; one who gives
Thomas: Twin
Benjamin: Son of the right hand
Joseph: He will add
Simon: He has heard
Achar: One who is troubled
Mary: Wished for child; sea for bitterness

CONTENTS

PRECIOUS MEMORIES

This is a story about a star, an infant's birth, and a woman named Esther. Caesar Augustus published a decree ordering a census of the whole world. Everyone went to register, each to his own town. So Joseph and his spouse Mary, who was with child, went to David's town of Bethlehem because he was of the house and lineage of David.

My husband, Jacob, and I are the proud proprietors of an inn. Our inn is located at the edge of the town of Bethlehem. On the first floor, we have our tavern, where meals and drinks are served. Tables and chairs fill the room.

At one end of the tavern is a large fireplace. It keeps the room warm on cold winter nights. Each day, the tavern offers our guests fresh bread that I have made and baked, roasted vegetables that are grown in our garden, and fine wine that Jacob made. On the second floor, there are several rooms where tired travelers can rest for the night.

Each room as a small window to allow fresh air to enter the room. There are hooks to hang their cloaks, and each room has a bowl and pitcher of water where guests may wash off the dust from the road. In the back of the inn are a corral and a manger where guests may stable, feed, and water their animals.

On the nearby hills, shepherds tend their flocks. Since the decree has gone out, our inn has been filled travelers from all over the country. Each night, every room has been filled. The tavern has served more meals than we ever thought possible. I have had to double my efforts at making and baking bread, and the pitchers of wine and trays of roasted vegetables seem to be leaving the kitchen in a constant stream of motion.

1

We no sooner get a patron fed and the table cleaned when there are new patrons to seat and feed. I'm not sure if it is the smell of bread being baked or the promise of fine-tasting wine that keeps the people coming. Nothing that we do for our patrons would be possible if it were not for our wonderful cook Rebecca and our skilled kitchen help Jessica, Mary, and Sarah—wonderful young women that I adore and love.

After a long day of labor and having all our guests fed and settled in for the night, Jacob and I often relax in our backyard. The cool night air is refreshing, and the night sky is filled with a million shining stars. As I gaze at the stars, I often wonder to myself how those heavenly bodies must show the glory and beauty of our creator.

Tonight, there appears to be one star that is outshining all the other stars. Its glimmering brilliance warms my heart, and I feel as if the heavenly host is touching the earth. As my husband and I prepare to settle down for a night's rest, there is a knock at the inn's door. When Jacob opens the door, before him stands a young man weary and tired from his day's travels. He has searched the entire town looking for lodging.

The man inquires if there are any rooms available. Jacob is about to send him away when I mention to Jacob that the wife is with child. With all the rooms that we have filled, all we can offer the couple is the use of our manger. It is a simple building: three walls, a roof, a feeding crib for the animals, and plenty of fresh straw. It will provide some protection from the cold night air.

I gather up some blankets, then Jacob and I show the young man Joseph and his wife, Mary, where our manger is located. Jacob and Joseph take fresh straw, spread it around, and then they make a place where the couple can rest. Then, they cover the straw with the blankets that I have brought. The animals from the yard seem to be drawn to the manger. They must sense something that we as humans fail to see.

My husband and I are getting ready to settle down to a much-needed rest when there is a loud and frantic knock on the door. Upon opening the door, to Jacob's surprise once again stood Joseph.

It seems that his wife has gone into labor. Jacob returns to our room to inform me of the pending birth. I quickly dress and retrieve the swaddling clothes that I once used for my children and accompany Joseph to the manger.

My experience as a midwife will surely come in handy this night. With the passing of time, the baby is born, a beautiful baby boy. I wrap the baby in the swaddling clothes and lay him next to his mother. The stillness of the night is broken by the sound of voices as they draw near the manger.

Shepherds have left their flocks because they have seen a great star in the night sky that is fixed over the manger. They tell us about heavenly beings dressed in brilliant white garments who have told them about the infant's birth. They share with us the words that men for ages have longed to hear: that the messiah, the bread of life, Emmanuel, has come to bring the good news to mankind.

WONDER AT THE JOURNEY'S END

Balthasar was at the beginning of his journey. He was on his way to—he didn't know where. It didn't matter. He was young and full of adventure, and this was his chance to follow his dreams. He had been looking at the night sky for so long, and last night, it happened.

The sign in the sky, he had longed to see. All his long hours of study were finally going to bring him some reward. He left his small town of Cyrene. With his bags filled with food, clothing, camping supplies, a small stash of coins that he had managed to save, and a small tin of frankincense just in case he needed something to barter with—everything he owned was packed.

With his heart full of wonder and his head fill of dreams, his journey began. After several weeks of travel, Africa and his small town seemed so very far away. As he sat by his campfire, he thought about his family, his mother, his father, his brother, and his little sister. He felt the chill of the night air and his loneliness creep in on him like a heavy fog.

As Balthasar sat by his small campfire, in the distance, he heard a strange sound. In an instance, all his senses were heightened as his ears strained to listen for further sounds in the blackness of the night. Out of the darkness, he heard the sound of voices asking if it was okay to share the comforts of his fire.

As the two men approached the dimness of the campfire out of the darkness of the night, they introduced themselves. The first man spoke with a foreign accent. His name was Caspar, and he was an astronomer from India. The second man introduced himself as

Melchior, a merchant from Arabia. As the two men sat down to warm themselves by the campfire, Balthasar introduced himself. He told the two that his given name was Balthasar, but his friends called him Simon. He hoped he had found two new friends.

As the night wore on, each man shared his story. Simon told his new friends how he had been a scholar in his town: how he started studying the night sky after reading in an ancient manuscript about a wondrous star that would appear before a great event. Caspar was excited when he heard Simon's words, for he had been studying the star.

It was the sighting of this star that started him on his journey. He told how he had sailed from Bombay across the Arabian Sea to the port of Abadan. It was on his voyage at sea that he met Melchior. Melchior shared how he had heard stories about the brilliant star from other wise men as he traveled about, doing his business. He shared how he had persuaded Caspar to allow him to travel along as his companion, for he, too, wanted to share in the excitement of this great event.

As the night slowly passed and the campfire died to glowing embers, each man drifted off to sleep. In the morning, it was decided that the three men would travel on together. As the days passed, they drew closer and closer to the star. It was almost within their grasp.

Simon told his companions how in an ancient text, he had read that in the town of Bethlehem, the great event was to happen. That a star, maybe their star, was foretelling of that event. In Hebrew, the town name was pronounced "Bet le hem," which meant house of bread. Maybe here, they would find the bread of life that they were seeking, and at long last, their journeys end. And now it is written.

Wise men came searching for something wonderful. They did not know what it was, but a beautiful star in the night sky foretold of the wondrous event. They had traveled far away from their homeland. They were hungry and tired, but they would not give up on their quest. The star they followed at last came to rest over a little house.

When they knocked upon the door, they were welcomed like family that had not been seen for a long time. Upon entering the home, they at long last gazed upon the wondrous event—a child. They had brought gifts: Simon had brought a tin of frankincense, Caspar had a bottle of myrrh, and Melchior a few gold coins from his purse. But more important than their gifts, each man had brought the gift of himself.

Foolish men would look at this child or any child and say, "It is only a child. What can it do? How can a child change the world?" But these were wise men. They say this child, unlike any child born before, would be the salvation of mankind. Children of every generation are the hope for the future of mankind. Maybe you think that this is the end of this story. No, this is only the beginning. For the quest is now yours. Your journey has just begun. It is now your assignment to seek out this special child for yourself.

SIMPLE MAN OF TRADE

As a young Jewish child, my days were filled with laughter, dreams, and fantasy. Childhood is so fleeting, and the dreams of yesterday seem to vanish like a mirage in the desert. Where is it written that once a young person is no longer a child, all dreams should end and the labors of life should be one's only reality?

My father has always been a hardworking man, and I'm proud to be able to work by his side. His skill as a master carpenter and furniture maker are unequaled in our village. His mastery is appreciated beyond our small village. My father's plans and desires are so innovative that customers come to him seeking his creative skills.

A rich merchant from a village near ours has contracted my father to build a luxurious and elaborate new house for him. Each morning, as we walk to work on this new project, I have seen a beautiful young woman drawing water from the village well with her mother. Why I have never noticed her before, I will never know.

Each day as we pass by, her beauty captivates me. In accordance with our customs and traditions, I have asked my father to see if a meeting can be arranged between our two families. At our first meeting, I learn that her name is Mary. I have been courting Mary for six months now. With each meeting, her grace and inner beauty reveal just how special a young woman she really is. During our courtship, my love for her has gown, and she has expressed her love for me.

With our families gathered, I have decided to ask Mary's father for her hand in marriage, and I have asked Mary if she would be my wife. Several weeks before our marriage, our mothers are busy preparing the banquet for our wedding day. Mary and I are also busy looking for a place to call our own. Our wedding day is just a week away, and I am filled with excitement and nervous tension as I think about Mary becoming my wife.

Several nights before Mary and I were to be wed, I had a dream where a handsome young man appeared to me and told me Mary was with child. I was awoken from my sleep by this disturbing nightmare because Mary and I had not yet expressed our physical love for one another. The next morning, as I walked to work, I met the young man that I had seen in my dream. Again, he told me that Mary was to bear a son and that we should name him Jesus.

He told me not to be afraid to wed Mary, that she was to be the mother of the Most High. Her son was to be the Messiah promised to Israel. As I traveled along the road with this young man, I knew it was not a dream. I spoke to him as one man speaks to another. I told him about my fears and how Mary and I would suffer the ridicule and scorn of the village. The women of the village would be counting the days from our marriage to the birth of the child. The young man assured me that with God, all things are possible: that Mary and I would not suffer the malicious gossip of the people in the village. With this final assurance, he vanished from my sight.

My love and trust in Mary's purity were reassured. I did take Mary as my wife. Shortly after we were married, we began our journey to Bethlehem where Mary was to give birth to her son. In Bethlehem, I found work as a carpenter and we settled down to life as a family, but our time here was to be short-lived.

Once again, the young man appeared to me and warned me of the impending danger that would soon befall the male children of this land. Like thieves in the night, Mary, her son, and I crept away from our new friends and the people that we had grown to love. After several long and difficult weeks of travel to Egypt, we once again settled down to family life.

I once again was able to find work and make a living for my family. Mary and I always wanted more children, but after the birth of her son, she was not able to conceive again. God must have heard our prayers and read the desire of our hearts. One morning, as I was walking to work, I heard an infant crying. I found a baby abandoned and hidden among the brambles alongside of the road. I returned home with the infant in my arms and explained to Mary how I had found the child. We accepted the child as our own, and we named him James. We raised the two boys as brothers.

THE BOY NEXT DOOR

Beyond our town is a whole new world to explore, and I intended to see that world just as soon as I grow up. My name is Jacob, and I live in the town of Galilee. I'm told it is not a big town, but the well in the center of town has cool, crisp sweet water. It tastes like honey melon that has sat in the shade all day.

I often help my mother as she draws water from the well. Some days, I draw from the well of living water. Our house is located near the center of town. My dad's bakery shop is in the front part of our house. Each morning, I am awakened by the smell of fresh bread being baked. The sweet aroma of Dad's bread is carried on the morning air. I'm sure that the whole town knows when bread is being baked.

Often, as I sit by the oven, warming myself from the crisp morning air, my father shares his knowledge with me. This morning, he told me that the ancient Egyptians use the word *Ish* for bread and for life because to them, bread meant life. My dad is an honest man. He charges a fair price for his day's labors. I'm sure that being a baker is an honorable trade, but I have dreams that reach beyond the walls of our town. Rabbi Esaw says that I am a daydreamer, that if I studied my lessons as hard as I played, a good student someday I could become.

Next door to our house is a broken-down little house. The front door is missing, the chimney leans, and there's a hole in the roof. The family that once lived there had to move because there was no work in town for the father. As I work on my chores and finish reading my lessons from the Torah, I hear activity outside. Someone is moving in next door.

The man seems to know what he is doing, for he is going about making repairs on the house. His wife is in the house, cleaning and making it ready for them to move in. The family donkey and cart are still loaded with all their possessions. On the cart are a table and chairs, bedding, cookware, tools, and a small bed. Please let there be someone my age I can play with.

It has been such a long time since I've had someone next door. Peeking out of the window, I discover there is a boy. He seems to be about my age, and he's working with his father. Maybe later, when they have moved in, I can play with him. I think I will go outside and let my presence be known. I've watched and waited all day long, but the boy and his father continued to make repairs on the house. As the last fingers of daylight reluctantly give way to the night, they finally quit working and go inside the house.

This has been one of the longest days I can remember. I find it hard to sleep, for tomorrow, I know the boy and I will meet. The next morning, as I sat in front of my house playing with my dreidel, my new neighbor came over and introduced himself. His name is Yeshua. In no time, we become the best of friends.

Yeshua loves to rough and tumble and play as much as I do. Our mothers go to the well each day to draw water together. The large earthen jars that they use when filled are heavy and cool as they walk along our dusty street back to our houses. Yeshua's father stops by my father's shop each night to buy bread for his family. I have come to regard Yeshua as my brother.

Yeshua attends the same school as me, but he seems to know things about life that I have not figured out yet. He and Rabbi Esaw often have long discussions about passages in the Torah. I have learned many lessons about life and the meaning of life from Yeshua. I guess the greatest lesson that I have learned is that we are free to choose our own path in life. I'm not really sure what I want to be when I grow up or what path I will follow.

Many years have passed since Yeshua and I played as children. He and his family moved away from our small town. I often think about my boyhood friend and wonder what path he has taken and how he has changed the world. As a young man, he often spoke to me about how one person could have a positive impact on humanity.

I have traveled many miles away from the walls of my small town in search of my destiny, the path I would follow. I have had my fair share of days when I longed to have a loaf of my father's bread and a drink of water from the town well—that cool, crisp water. After a wasted youth, I now believe that I have found what I want now that I have grown up. My search for my destiny has led me back to words my childhood friend Yeshua spoke to me: one man can make a difference. I am studying to become a rabbi. I believe that I can best serve my fellow man by sharing my thirst for truth and my willingness to face my own faults.

LIFE WITH PURPOSE

Few men are born knowing what their purpose in life will be. My destiny was written before I was born. I was not born into wealth or greatness. I was born to serve one much greater than I. From my earliest memories, I can recall how my younger cousin and I played together as children. Our mothers acted more like sisters than cousins. They watched over us as we played as intensely as a mother hen watched over her chicks.

Early each morning, our mothers would go down to the well in the center of our town to draw water. As our mothers labored to fill stone jars with fresh water, my cousin and I played in the cool water that splashed on to the warm stones that surrounded the well. With the morning chore completed, our mothers prepared our midday meal.

After we finished eating our meal, we were sent off to the temple. Lessons from the Torah are taught to all the village children by my father. He does his best to explain the meaning of passages found in the scrolls. Most of the time, his explanations fail to answer our simple questions. Often, he forgets that we are just children and not great scholars. What I have learned from this experience is that, quite often, learned men and scholars fail to comprehend the simplicity of God's message to mankind.

My father hopes that someday, I will follow in his footsteps as a priest. I love my father and don't want to disappoint him, but I need to find my own purpose in life. My cousin and I have both grown strong in body, mind, and spirit. I often work with my uncle Joseph in his carpentry shop. His skilled hands are rough and calloused, yet his kind and gentle ways have helped to form me into the man I am today.

After a long day of working in the shop, Aunt Mary and my mom often prepare a meal for all of us to enjoy: fire-roasted fish, fresh baked bread, and cool refreshing water for parched lips and sweet dates for dessert. A meal made with loving hands always hits the spot.

Life has a strange way of changing young boys into men, and for each, the journey is different. After my mother Elizabeth and my father Zechariah passed away, I spent a long time in the wilderness searching, praying, and fasting. I wandered about lost, a man without purpose. I survived on locust and wild honey. I forgot about my relatives and my cousin that loved me like a brother, and I mourned for the loss of my parents.

It is strange how solitude can bring such clarity of mind. The next morning, I walked out of the wilderness and into a life of preaching lessons that my father had taught me long ago. I started baptizing people in the river Jordan, and many came to be baptized and to prepare themselves for the coming of the Messiah. One day, among the crowd of people stood the cousin that I loved. Out of his love for me, he asked that I baptize him. With his baptism, I came to understand his role and mine in God's great plan for mankind.

My cousin, the stepson of a carpenter, was to become the greatest teacher that the world would ever know. As for myself, John, I was to become one heralding the way of the Lord. I have discovered that the treasure in life is not always in the finding of priceless stones and precious metals. The true treasure in life is in the seeking, searching, and the enlightenment that follows.

WATER FOR HER SOUL

Anna is the oldest woman that comes to the well each day. We all wait for her anticipated arrival. She moves slowly along the dusty road of our town with her bowed legs, crooked walking stick, and small water jar. Old and young women, even children, wait for Anna's arrival. All know that she is the town's storyteller.

Her stories always bring back memories for the older women, pique the interest of the younger women, and entertain the children. Her stories are about a time long forgotten by the younger generation, a time when our town was but a small village and first inhabited by the Samaritan people. As she settles down in her favorite place to sit, the children gather around. All eyes are fixed on her, and all listen intently for her story to begin.

Today, Anna has chosen to tell us about the early days of our town: days when farmers and merchants first settled in the small village, a time when the hills around the village were covered in wheat. She shares her memories of when the wind moved over the wheat fields. It looked like golden waves dancing on the hillsides, a picture we can only imagine, for the hillsides have long ago given way to the ever-expanding housing.

"There was a time in my life," Anna explains, "when this old woman you see before you was a young and happily married wife, a time when love and youth filled my working day with happiness."

Everyone who visits the well knows that she has been divorced several times. Her older acquaintances have strayed away, but her true friends know of the trials and tribulations that she has endured. When I was a young woman, I came early in the morning like the other women of our village. All the women, old and young, gathered at the well much like we do today.

We shared in the drawing of water and the filling of water jars. Lowering the bucket and raising it again is difficult work, but many hands make the task much easier. It was a much happier time. There was a time for talking and singing and the sharing of the problems of raising children. The older women often had advice on how children should be raised; the younger women listened intently to their solutions and questioned their logic.

There is a momentary pause as she gathers her thoughts and begins her story once again. She recalls a time when a young Jewish traveling teacher came to the village. She had heard that He was teaching about a new way of living and praying to God. He said that we are all children of his Father and we are free to love God and give Him honor and praise as we see fit.

She wished she could go and listen to his teachings, but Jews and Samaritans had no dealings with one another. She knew in her heart of hearts that the truth is the truth no matter where it comes from if the man is truly a man of God. She recalled how one day, as she was drawing water from the well, the young teacher came and sat down by the well. She was startled when He asked her if she could give Him a drink of water from her jar.

She looked around the square to see if any eyes were looking at them, for she was already a woman scorn by the villagers. With trembling hands, she withdrew a metal cup from her wrap and filled it with the cool refreshing water from her jar and gave it to Him to drink. He sat in silence as he slowly took in the surroundings and drank the water. She wanted to question where He got His authority to teach as He did among the people, but fear kept the words in her mouth and her tongue from moving.

As if he could see down through the years of her life and the questions of her mind, He knew her heart's desires and the secrets of her soul. He took another swallow of the water and began to speak to her. He told her that no matter what others may think of her, His father in heaven loves her. She looks into His eyes and sees the love and compassion that she has not found in any man's arms.

He tells her that the love she sees is only a reflection of the love that His father has for her. As tears swell up in her eyes, she asks if there is a place in heaven for a woman who has lived a life like hers. The young teacher tells her that His father has sent Him here to assure mankind that there is a place for all His children at His banquet table, that His father is a loving God and does not send any of His children away hungry.

The thirst and hunger that she has endured in this life can be quenched with the words of truth that He teaches, for His teachings are the good news that mankind has longed to hear. As her story ends with these last few words, Anna is quiet as if she is reliving being in the presence of the young teacher.

Anna has told this story countless times during the years of her life, and it has never changed. She feels the love of God her father and knows with every fiber of her being, that this young teacher has set her spirit free, and that Gods love is more than human words and emotions can express.

ACTS OF LOVE

All my life, I have heard about the pool of Bethesda and the five colonnades made of beautiful white stone that surround it. Bethesda is called the house of mercy because of the wonders that happen within its pool.

During the heat of the day, I love to lean on a stone colonnade and feel the coolness of the stone against my skin. My name is Machlown in Hebrew. My name means one who is sick. Day after day, I'm brought here by members of my family. They bring me here before they go to work in the fields to tend the crops.

I, like many others, are left here. We are the crippled, the disfigured, the blind, and the mute. We are all here, children of the God who created us as we are. We are all hoping that today an angel of God will stir the water and those of us who enter the pool will be healed of our afflictions. My legs ache, and my body is racked with pain. My mind and my soul cry out each day for mercy. I pray to the God of Israel, the God of our Father Abraham, to accept me Lord just as I am: sinful, broken, battered, and bruised. I will not allow myself to be overcome with self-pity, for hope still burns bright within my spirit.

Every day, a crowd of people walk by my litter: rich merchants, Pharisees, Sadducees, Roman soldiers, and common people. Sometimes, a rich merchant or a Roman soldier will be moved with compassion, and they will place a coin on my litter. They are unlike men from the Sanhedrin who are interpreters of the law and teachers of the law. They stand in judgment wondering what sins my father and mother or my ancestors committed that caused me to be condemned to this crippled body.

Some people look at me with compassion in their eyes and pity on their faces, while others look at my misshapen body in discussed. In this house of mercy, there is one who practices mercy every day. Her name is Dalit. As the heat of the day intensifies, she arrives with her son Isaac. They give all of us cool refreshing water to quench our parched throats. It is a true act of kindness given without expectation.

I can hear the voices of a large gathering of people entering the area. They all seem to be following a young man. As they draw closer, I recognize some of them. They are priests, scribes, and members of the Sanhedrin. Some of the people in the crowd call the young man rabbi while others call him master.

As he approaches where I lay upon my litter, he bends down to look into my eyes. He asks me if I believe that salvation will come from the Jews. I answer that I await the coming of the messiah promised to our people. He replied that in my seeing him, that promised has been fulfilled: that the God of Abraham has heard my prayer and has sent his son to answer that prayer.

In an instant, my crooked legs were made straight and strong. I stood at once, giving thanks to God for His mercy and love. When I turned around to thank the young rabbi, he was already swallowed up by the crowd.

IDENTICAL BUT DIFFERENT

My name is David. I am Thomas's twin and older brother. I was born a full three minutes before he made his appearance. Even as an infant, Thomas was reluctant to leave the comfort and safety of the womb. I was named after a great, noble, and fearless king of the Israelites. My brother Thomas was named after an uncle who never married and was cautious with every penny he made.

Father told me as toddlers that I was the first to walk. I took my first steps without hesitation, ready to explore the world. My brother held on to father's hands, questioning his balance, weary of his next step. Even though my brother and I look alike, our attitude about life is very different. I seek adventure and excitement, the thrill of each new challenge the beginning of each new day.

I want to taste the entire flavor and smell all the aromas that life has to offer. My brother Thomas is happy and content to live in the security of familiar surroundings. He is fearful of new and unfamiliar thoughts and ideas. Adventure for my brother is using the family mikvah to prepare for the Sabbath. I was surprised when he told me about a young rabbi named Jesus, that he and a friend had been following and listening to his teachings. Venturing this far out of his safety zone has never been a part of Thomas's lifestyle.

He told me that this young rabbi was teaching the people about a new way of viewing and thinking about one another: not as master or slave, not as Gentile or Jew, but as brothers and sisters and to respect one another as our Father—the God of Abraham, Isaac, and Jacob—loves us, His sons and daughters.

Such thoughts and teachings are so far from the social norms, they should have frightened my brother, yet Thomas seemed to embrace these new teachings. Day after day, he followed this young teacher. He witnessed wonders and signs that confused his mind and baffled his senses. I know that many of you have heard that seeing is believing, and for some, this is true. But for my brother Thomas, seeing only left him with more unanswered questions.

As for myself, seeing is only the first step in the quest to bring logic to a confusing and at times baffling world—a life for ups and downs, truths and deceptions that must be sorted out. I love my brother Thomas, yet there are times when I wonder why we are not more alike in our lives. As for myself, why am I not more cautious? And for Thomas, why is he not a little more adventurous?

There is a beautiful young woman that I have seen at the town well in the morning. I would like to meet her. Her beauty and grace captivate me. I have tried many times to speak with her, but each time I approach, my tongue and self-confidence fails me. The words that I wish to say will not leave my mouth. This woman makes me doubt all that I think I know. For what man can understand the thoughts of a woman? Women baffle me. I have been told by other men that the confusion about women started with the first man and woman. My curiosity and inner man compel me to keep trying to move past my fear and have faith in the goodness of this young woman.

Faith is an inner experience that my brother Thomas may never know. Faith is like a mirage on the desert. You can see it in your mind's eye, or you can logically think it away. One day, I hope that I may have the courage to engage in a conversation with the young woman that I have admired from afar.

SEEKING TRUTH

I was born a child with an inquisitive mind. At a very young age, I developed a very analytic mind. I tested all things in my life. I wanted to see things as they were and not as I wished them to be. You may recall the childhood game of hide-and-go-seek. For me, it was more than a game, for my whole life has been a quest to seek answers to many questions that are hidden from the wisest of men.

For many of my years, I have followed the discipline of science. All things need to be proven and logically make sense. I have studied the stars, nature, and my fellow man. I find it fascinating to observe nature and wonder why all things in nature act as they do, and why do human beings act so foolishly at certain times?

My mind makes me question why the stars stay in the sky and exactly what they are. I know that the seasons change, but what exactly tells the leaves on the trees to change color and what tells the grass to grow in the spring? Why do some of my fellow humans have dark skin and others lighter skin, and why did the almighty create women?

Questions, questions. So few answers and so little time. I can only hope that I unlock some of the answers before my time on earth has expired.

One day, as I was sitting by the Sea of Galilee deep within thought, I was interrupted by a large gathering of people that were following this young rabbi. I come to this quiet spot to be alone with my thoughts; but this large mob of people all around me are talking about miraculous cures: blind men seeing again, lame individuals walking and running, and lepers being made whole and clean again. These words made me want to investigate what they were talking about. These things I had to see with my own eyes, hear with my ears, and touch with my hands. It was hard for me to imagine that broken bodies could be made whole.

As the crowd of people passed by me, one more was added to their numbers. I made sure that I followed at a safe distance not too far back so I couldn't see and hear what was happening. We were all walking along when suddenly, the young teacher stopped, and I heard him proclaim in a loud clear voice above the din of the crowd. "Who touched me?"

A sudden silence fell over the crowd. No one moved a muscle or spoke a word. In my mind, I answered His question in an instance, but my lips did not move. You are in a crowd surrounded by people. Everyone is pushing and shoving to get close to you. Before my thoughts had time to clear the air, an old woman stepped out of the crowd and told the teacher it was she who touched the hem of his garment.

The young teacher looked at her and told her to go her way, for her faith has made her clean. What did I miss? What did He mean her faith has made her clean? Faith? What is faith? You can't touch it, hold it in your hands, or even see it.

Faith is like the will-o'-the-wisp. As the crowd starts to move again, I hear murmuring among the people. A whisper passes from one person to the next. The old woman has been unclean for many years. She has a condition of blood. As I walked along, I wonder why this old woman believed that this young rabbi could somehow help her. What did she witness that I failed to see?

I must be more observant. I need to move closer to the front, closer to the young rabbi. As I make my way to the front of the mob of people, I hear more stories about withered hands being made a new, the dead rising from the grave, and multitudes of people being fed with only a few loaves of bread and a few fish. I at last have made my way to the front. I'm only a few feet away from the teacher when suddenly, he stops and turns around and addresses me.

"Didymas Thomas," He calls me by my name. "Come and follow me, and I will show you more wonders than you could ever imagine." So I did as He had requested. I followed Him, and I have witnessed healings and wonders that defy scientific explanation. Water turned into wine, eyes that were once dark now filled with the light of day, and limbs that were once broken and deformed made whole by the touch of His hand. Day after day, throngs of people came to Him. And He cured them all. Gentile or Jew, master or slave—He never judges. He only acts out of love and compassion for all of them.

For several weeks, I, Thomas, have now followed the teacher; and I have seen, have heard, and have touched with my hands. Yet I am still not convinced that what I perceive with my senses is real. There has to be a reasonable explanation!

All my questions, He answers like a father teaching a child. He knows me, He senses my doubt, and He comforts me with these words. "Thomas, many a wise man has longed to hear what you have heard, and many have longed to see what you have seen. Do not doubt any longer but believe in me."

MY BROTHER'S KEEPER?

It is time that I, Kefir, told my story. I'm sure you have all heard my younger brother's story, the prodigal son. If I sound somewhat bitter in my telling of my story, I feel I have a right to be. Before my younger brother was born, I was the favorite son of my father.

Being the oldest and firstborn of several children was an envied position, but with great honor comes many responsibilities. At a young age, I was charged with watching over my father's herd of goats. Each morning, I would lead them out to green pastures, and each evening, I would lead them back to the safety of their pens.

Father waited many years for his favorite wife to have a baby boy. This was the beginning of my downward slide from favorite son. Our father doted on Reuben like he was his only child. My sisters and I tended to our father's crops along with his servants.

Each day, as we labored in the fields, our brother stood at father's side. On Ruben's eighteenth birthday, father threw a lavish party and, as a gift, placed an eloquent ring on his finger, an elaborately made robe on his shoulders, and finely made sandals on his feet.

Father never asked Reuben to help in the fields or tend his herds like the rest of us children did. He never had to soil his hands with the menial tasks that need to be done on the farm. Two years after his eighteenth birthday, Reuben asked father for his share of the inheritance. As he walked away from the house with his purse bulging with coins, I was too busy working to even notice that he had left. The day-to-day routine of the farm continued uninterrupted. At the end of the day, I often found our father standing in the doorway, looking down the road and weeping.

My friends who had been to town have informed me of my brother's debauchery: how he is the life of the party, buying drinks and ladies of the evening for his newfound friends. Many weeks have passed, and I have not heard any news about my brother. There are still evenings when I find our father still standing in the doorway, looking down the road to the house.

As much as I dislike my brother, my father's tears have started to melt my icy heart. Don't misunderstand my intentions; I still believe my brother is a spoiled brat. Tomorrow, I must travel to the town where I heard my brother is living. I have meetings with local merchants. Our crops are ready to harvest, and I am in hopes I can sell them all. During my stay in town, father has asked me to check on Reuben, but I pray he has moved on and our paths will not cross. My second day in town is a very fruitful and profitable day. My meetings with the town merchants have gone well. I was able to sell all our crops.

I am on the outskirts of town when I see a young man feeding pigs. As I draw closer to the pig pens, at first, I do not recognize the young man. His clothes are filthy, his hands and face are dirty, and there are no sandals on his feet. Upon a closer look, I feel a sickening pain in the pit of my stomach as I recognize my brother.

His life of hedonism and debauchery has left him in this miserable state. My feelings of anger and lack of love for Reuben have not changed, but I remind myself that he is my brother. I offer to buy him a meal, a night's lodging, a bath and remind him that he has a loving father. The next day, I once again start on my journey home.

When I arrive home, I do not have the heart to tell our father about the sorry state in which I found my brother. Several weeks have passed since my visit to town. Each evening, father still stands in the doorway, looking longingly down the road, waiting for his prodigal son to return.

A FAVOR OWED

For several days now, the whole Sanhedrin has been discussing and arguing over the rumored teachings of a man named Jesus who has been instructing the people. As each day passes, a new rumor is heard about His teaching, and given new life, they spread like wildfire amongst the elders of the temple.

The elders wring their hands, rend their garments, and curse under their breath. They shout and curse the outright vanity. The gall of this young upstart to think he knows more about the God of Israel than the wise and learned men of the whole Sanhedrin. The situation has reached a fevered pitch when I, Joseph of Aramathia, offer my services to check out the teachings of this Jesus. As a member of the Sanhedrin and respected businessman, it is my personal belief that the best way to get to know the character of a man is to place him in a social situation then closely observe his behavior.

My daughter is engaged to a man whose family lives in Cana. In two weeks' time, they are to be married. The father of the groom has asked my wife and I if the wedding feast can take place in Cana. All his sons have had their wedding feast in the beautiful gardens on the family estate. So my wife and I journey to Cana to check out the gardens.

The estate gardens are very elegant. There are large stands of olive trees where guests can rest in the shade away from the heat of the day. The perfume of sweet jasmine fills the air, and cool breezes wash down over the gardens, making this a true oasis.

Messengers are sent throughout the towns and villages. All are invited. Jesus, His mother, and His disciples are welcome guests. All the preparations for the wedding feast have been made. I believe that the wedding feast has gone off without a hitch. I did not know that there was a problem with the wine until the head servant, Ofa, told me that the wine had run out. And he and the other servants were asked by Jesus to fill the water jars, then bring a cup of the liquid to the wine steward for tasting.

I am not sure how I missed this event happening, for I kept a sharp eye on this particular guest. After this oversight on my part, I was determined to keep a much closer watch and do further investigation.

On the second day of the week, I joined the throng of people who had gathered to listen to the teachings of this man called Jesus. I disguised my appearance by wearing simple clothing. As I sat and listened to His teachings, I did not hear Him say anything offensive. He talked about the God of Israel as if He had a personal relationship with Him.

As I walked home that day, I could not help but ponder the words that were spoken throughout Jesus's teaching. Tomorrow is a new day, and once again, I will sit and listen carefully to the teaching of the man called Jesus. For me, there will be no more whispered rumors, only the truth that I have heard with my own ears. This morning, Jesus has chosen to speak on the subject of life after death. His words are on a subject that will be welcomed by us Pharisees but not by all the Sanhedrin. Sadducees do not believe in life after death and believe it is wrong to fill the minds of simple men with nonsense about an afterlife.

I have listened to many teachings over the past two weeks. It was after one of Jesus's teachings that I lingered to talk with Him, but before I could speak, He asked me what it was that I was seeking. I told Him that I wanted to know where He got His authority to teach as He had been doing. After this first meeting, we spent many nights discussing lessons in the Torah. Sometimes, our discussions lasted into the early morning hours.

Each time I left one of our meetings, I could not help but wonder about Jesus's knowledge and understanding. He made each lesson and each verse come alive and its meaning crystal clear. As the hours became days and the days became precious memories of time spent with a friend, my respect for the man became stronger and my preconceived judgment became a thing of the past.

I know that my findings will not be well received by the members of the Sanhedrin, but I must tell them the truth of what I have discovered—that the man that they feared did not teach any false doctrine. His teachings supported the beliefs of the Jewish religion.

BANQUET FOR A WEDDING

My name is Ofa. I am a servant in the house of my master. I am writing down this story so it will not be lost in the passing of time. This story is not about myself but is about something wonderful. My master wished to hold a great wedding banquet for his oldest son.

Extra cooks, bakers, and laborers were brought in to help with the feast. The best of the master's livestock were taken to the butcher. Two young calves, five lambs, twenty geese, and the forty chickens were prepared for the banquet. Bakers were busy in the kitchen, baking large numbers of sweet breads soaked in the finest of honey. The aroma of baking bread and honey filled the air.

Cooks prepared fruits on large trays: figs, dates, apples, oranges, and pomegranates that tantalized the pallet and whet the appetite. Labors were sent out through the countryside to purchase and gather all manner of flowers. Wine merchants from the region were contacted and asked to bring their finest wines to the master's house. For days before the banquet, camels laden with large earthen vessels arrived.

Messengers were sent throughout the town, to villages and the countryside, to invite all to the banquet. No one was to be left uninvited.

Tables and places to sit were set up in the olive grove where, under the olive trees, guests could sit in the shade and comfort away from the midday sun.

As guests arrived, servants removed their sandals, and the dust from the road was washed from their feet. After this customary gesture, all were greeted by the master and his wife, their son, and his new wife. Guests were dressed in their finest wedding clothes. Many brought gifts for the young couple. Among the invited guests was a young rabbi. He arrived with his mother and his followers.

Music filled the air, and the sweet perfumed fragrance of flowers washed over the guests. All the food which had been prepared was brought before the guests. Servants were asked to tend to every need of the invited guests.

There was music and dancing and food aplenty. It was my job as the head servant to keep an eye on the wine. It was past midday when I noticed that the wine was running low. I was talking to one of the other servants when the mother of the young rabbi overheard my concern about the lack of wine.

I was more than embarrassed and mystified when the young rabbi asked me if I could have the six stone jars used for foot washing refilled with water. My fellow servants and I did as He had requested. When all the jars were filled, He went and sat with His mother. I could not hear what He said to His mother, but anyone with eyes that see could not mistake the love that passed between mother and son.

After a short discussion, the young rabbi came over and asked me to bring a pitcher of water to the head steward. With fear and trembling, I poured the water into the steward's glass. Much to my amazement, its appearance was as red as wine. I doubted my own eyes. I do not know how this happened, but I'm convinced that the young rabbi had something to do with this wondrous event.

I hurried back to the where the water jars were stored for now. I wanted to taste this water which had been changed to wine. My eyes did not deceive me, and my taste buds conceived my doubting foolish mind that this was the finest wine that I had ever tasted. I have heard the young rabbi called the Messiah. From what I have seen and now know, I, Ofa, now have a new master to follow. For His yoke is easy and His load is light, and all my transgressions He has taken away.

LESSON LEARNED

Benjamin Smallstien was small in stature; but by no means was he small in dreams, deeds, or generosity. He was much shorter than all the other boys in the village. With a name like Smallstien, what did he expect? The boys in the village nicknamed him smalls.

Other boys had growth spurts where they seemed to shoot up a few inches every month. Benjamin had growth fizzles, as he liked to call them, where he added only fractions of an inch to his height. He often dreamed of growing four or five inches. If he wanted to follow in his father's footsteps as a baker, he would need this additional height. At his present height, the opening to his father's ovens were still out of his reach.

Benjamin loved to sit in his father's bakery in the early morning. The aroma of fresh bread as it baked washed over him like a warm wave igniting his sense of smell. The bakery was his favorite place to sit and dream of possibilities. If he just grew five inches, someday, he could become a carpenter, a shepherd, or a shopkeeper. In his wildest dream, he longed to grow tall enough to become a soldier.

Lost in his dreams, Benjamin had forgotten his reason for being in the bakery. His father soon awakened him from his dream state. The bread had finished baking, and it was time for him to start his daily deliveries. With the bread still hot from the oven, Benjamin loaded his basket and set off on his way.

His first stop is at the rabbi's house. A gentle knock on the door, and the rabbi's wife answered the door. She is a kind and gentle woman who always thanks Benjamin for the loaf of bread as he hands it to her. She places a coin in his hand as payment, and he puts it in his money purse. His next stop is at the local inn.

The innkeeper always insists on selecting the three loaves of bread that the inn will use. He looks carefully at each loaf of bread. After his selection is made, he pays for the bread then hurries off to other areas of the inn. He is always into much of a hurry for even a kind word. The next stop on his route is at the tailor's shop.

The tailor is a rather large and robust man. His smile and personality seem to fill up a room with laughter and true joy. The tailor pays for his loaf of bread with a few small coins. His next-to-last stop is down by the lake where a local fisherman receives his loaf of bread and makes his payment with two fishes from the day's catch.

Benjamin's last stop is by far his favorite. Each day, he carries in his basket a small loaf of bread. This he brings to the front gate of his village to give to the old man that sits there, begging. He cannot explain in words why this small act of kindness brings him such great pleasure. The old man always thanks him for the bread and promises to pray for him and his parents.

Benjamin's mother and father have instilled in him the value of being generous. From a very young age, his parents taught him two life lessons to live by. Lesson one: For those who have much, much is expected. Lesson two: When you cast your bread on the water, it comes back to you a hundredfold.

The first lesson was easy to understand, for there was always bread in his house to eat. The second lesson was much harder to understand. One time, he took some bread and threw it in the lake near the village, and all it did was sink. The negative results of this experience only added to his confusion. What was the real meaning of this lesson? Benjamin wondered.

At each of his stops on his route, today, people were talking about a young rabbi named Jesus who was teaching the people. He was instructing the people to love one another as their Father in heaven loved them, to show compassion to those who have less than they themselves have.

With all the curiosity of a young child, Benjamin wanted to hear for himself what else this Jesus had to say. He sat at a distance from the great crowd as he listened intently to the words that this young rabbi proclaimed to the people gathered there.

It was about time for the midday meal when some of the rabbi's disciples came through the crowd seeking food. Benjamin offered to the disciples the five loaves and two fishes he had left in his basket. He watched with interest to see what the young rabbi whom they called Jesus would do with so little to feed so many.

Jesus lifted the basket above his head and, in a loud prayer, gave thanks for the bounty that was given and asked his Father to bless the bread and fish. He then gave the basket to his disciples, and they passed the bread and fishes out to the multitude of people that had gathered.

When all had eaten their fill, the disciples then gathered up the scraps of food that was left, and it filled twelve baskets. When Benjamin saw with his own eyes what had just happened, the understanding and meaning of the second lesson was revealed to him.

A MEAL FIT FOR A KING

For many years, my father has run the finest tavern and inn in all of Jerusalem. If this sounds a bit prideful, I guess I am, for I now am in charge of running this fine old establishment. It has always been the policy of our inn to offer our guests the finest in fine dining.

We import the best wines from around the area. We buy only the choicest cuts of meats, and we purchase the freshest fruits and vegetables. I believe that our success in business is due to our care and diligence. The inn is always crowded with local villagers, and travelers from far and wide have heard about our excellent food. Our chef is a master in the kitchen, and few besides myself are his equal.

Each day, we search the marketplace and buy the freshest of ingredients to prepare the day's meals. After the morning shopping is completed, the kitchen ovens are heated, fresh bread is baked, and it is so delightful it would be the envy of any woman. From early morning until the last evening's meal is served, the kitchen is alive with the sound of clattering plates and a mire of intoxicating aromas.

Fridays are exceptionally busy at the inn. Most of the villagers are preparing for the Sabbath. Many have asked our kitchen to cook meats that will be used for the Sabbath meal. It has always been our tradition to cook these meats for the villagers since our ovens are heated from first light until the dark of night.

As guests enjoy a meal in our inn, it has always been my habit to mingle with them and check on their satisfaction with their meal and the service that they have received. Most of the time, as I move from table to table, the conversation is only polite prattle and idle gossip. The conversations are almost always the same: trouble on the job or trouble with the in-laws. Most often heard is trouble with the children, and where the respect for other people that we learned as children has gone. Everyone is in such a hurry that it seems like common courtesy is lost.

I recognize some of our regular customers, and I go over to their table to see if they are satisfied with their meal. While I am engaged in conversation with them, they tell me about a young rabbi that they have been following. They have been listening to His teachings and feel that I could benefit from the words that He speaks. When I question them about where I might go and listen to him teach, they inform me that He will be speaking at the synagogue on the Sabbath.

I can only wonder what words He could speak that will be inspirational to me. Being from the food industry, I believe that the best way to judge another man's meal is to go and give his food a try, and I think the best way to judge a man's teaching is to go and listen to what He has to say. So that is exactly what I did.

On the Sabbath, I went and listened to what this young rabbi had to say. He read a passage from the Torah, then He looked at all that were gathered and said, "In your hearing, I am the fulfillment of this Old Testament scripture." With these few words, more than a few eyebrows were raised. My curiosity and desire to hear more of His teachings were only heightened by His last statement.

The next day, I did not need to go to work, so I went out and followed the young rabbi.

The words that He spoke during that day only whet my appetite for more of His teachings. I witnessed in His manner more compassion and understanding than I had ever seen in any man. Crowds of people flocked to be with him. They brought Him their sick, and He cured their ills with the touch of His hands. And with the words from His lips, He mended their broken spirits, and all that He spoke came to be.

One among us asked Him how we were to pray. He taught us to say, "Our Father who art in heaven holy is thy name. Thy kingdom come, thy will be done on earth as it is in heaven. Give us our daily bread and forgive us our trust passes as we forgive those who trust pass against us and lead us not into temptation but deliver us evil."

This prayer left many of us with a multitude of thoughts to fill our minds. Never had I thought to call God my Father, and the idea of forgiving others was new idea to me.

Monday morning came as I started back to work. My mind was filled with questions. I could hardly concentrate on the job at hand. It was one of the longest days that I have had in my life. The words of the young rabbi echoed in my mind over and over.

In a few days, we will be celebrating Passover. Much to my surprise, two of the disciples of the young rabbi have come to my establishment to reserve a room for the Passover meal to be celebrated. I am excited, and I show them an eloquent banquet area that we have in an upper room.

I know that the young teacher will be part of their celebration, so I want to prepare a meal fit for a king. I ask the kitchen staff to choose the finest wines and cook the Passover lamb with the greatest of skill.

As I greet the young rabbi and his followers, He invites me to join Him and His followers in their celebration. I accept His invitation; and sometime during the meal, the teacher takes bread, gives thanks, and breaks the bread. He says, "This is my body."

In like manner, He takes the cup of wine, gives thanks, and says, "This is my blood given for you and for all for the forgiveness of sins. Do this in memory of me." After we had shared this meal, all the words that He had spoken and all of the things that I had seen and heard touched my heart. I, Joseph, have left my father and mother to follow Him wherever He may lead. For my heart's desire is to please my Lord.

NATURE'S REVERENCE

As a young sapling, I was planted in this garden the same year that the Master/Creator chose to come to earth. As each year passes, I have gown taller, and my limbs reach higher into the sky. My roots creep deeper into the ground, anchoring me to the earth.

In the thirteenth year of my life, I can recall when the young Master/Creator came to the garden for the first time to pray. I remember how excited all of nature seemed to be, how the blades of grass all pushed up from the soil so they could create a carpet for His feet to walk upon, how all the flowers in the garden raised their heads up and expelled their fragrance to perfume the air He would breathe. I recall how the birds filled my branches to sing their sweet songs and how all the trees in the garden bent our limbs down in reverence to shade and protect our Creator from the heat of the sun.

Every time that the Master comes to the garden to pray, the symphony of nature is replayed. With each passing day, the wind whispers through the leaves on my limbs and throughout the garden, heralding the wondrous deeds that the Master is doing for man. With each time that the Master/Creator comes to the garden, the olives within my branches become sweeter as they recognize the beauty of their Creator. The nectar that is extracted from them is the most aromatic and deepest golden color.

In the thirty-third year of my life in this garden called Gethsemane, I remember when the Master once again came to the garden to pray. Unlike times in the past, this time, all of nature sensed the heaviness in our Creator's heart.

The grass, the flowers, the birds, the air, and all trees in the garden felt the bitter anguish in our Master/Creator's prayers.

As He prayed through the night, the grass withered in shame. The beauty of the flowers faded, the birds in my limbs sang songs of sorrow, the air became heavy with grief, and the leaves on all trees dropped like tears.

I have recorded all the events that happened this night around the rings of my heart. My recollection is so very clear, for this is the night when my life changed and I became a weeping willow.

SIMON'S STORY

My story begins on one starry, starry night many years ago when I was a much younger man. A bright star in the night sky beckoned me to follow. I listened to that inner calling, and what I found has made all the difference in my life. So I began my journey to a foreign land.

The journey was long, and I encountered many hardships along the way. There were many times when I wanted to give up and end this foolish trip. Each night, as I made camp and lay beneath the sky, that glorious star kept calling my name; and with the dawn of each new day, the wind whispered in my ears, "Come, come and see." Each day, I was driven by an inner desire that grew even stronger to go and seek the secrets of the star and discover what treasure lay shrouded in its glow.

As I traveled on, I found fellow travelers—men like myself from foreign lands in search of answers to the beckoning of the star to come and see. My fellow seekers and I traveled on for many days together. Each night as we made camp, we sat by the campfire's glow and questioned one another about what wondrous treasures we would find. Our combined knowledge told us that this star, this glorious star, was heralding something great; for this was the first time in all of written or verbal history that the heavens had ever put on such a magnificent display.

After several weeks of travel, our journey and our seeking came to an end in the small town of Bethlehem. Many people were gathered at the place where the star overshadowed and cast down its heavenly rays. There were shepherds from nearby fields, fathers and mothers and their children from the town, and there were shopkeepers. Many were called to come and see, but some were too busy with their own pursuits. Others chose to ignore the inner voice, that whisper from the star.

When I first saw the Christ child, I could see in His face the pure Shekinah glory of God. In less than an instant, I knew that I had found a treasure beyond measure, and I knelt along with the others in reverence to the living Son of God. Many who were gathered brought gifts in homage to the Christ child.

I, in turn, presented my gift to the child. This would be my first gift, and little did I know that it would not be my last. After all the gifts were given, many left and returned their homes. As for me, I felt compelled by some deep inner force to stay and watch as the young child grew. My hometown of Cyrene was so very far away, and my desire to stay and watch the child became the focus of my life. The many skills that I possessed allowed me to stay in the towns where He and His family lived.

I was there with the elders of the temple when the Christ child gave a teaching on the meaning of the scriptures. All that heard His teaching were amazed at the wisdom and depth of His understanding. He answered all the elders' questions with knowledge far beyond the abilities of a child.

I watched and observed the boy as He grew from childhood to young adult and manhood, and I stood in wonder as I saw Him grow spiritually and love for His fellow man. As He began His ministry of teaching and healing the sick, my own love for this Son of God only became stronger.

At the wedding feast in Cana, I witnessed firsthand the love that God the Father has for His only begotten Son as His Son changed water into wine.

I followed the young teacher as He made His triumphant ride into the city of Jerusalem, and I was in the Praetorium courtyard when the people He loved so dearly turned on Him and screamed for His death. I wept bitter tears as I walked with Him as He carried His cross to Golgotha. I was standing in a doorway along the narrow street when I watched Him fall a third time beneath the weight of the cross.

It was at this time that a Roman soldier forced me to help Him carry His cross. I felt more than pleased to help Him carry that cross, for I had one last gift to give Him. I had already given Him my heart on that special night in Bethlehem, and I considered it an honor to give Him the strength in my body.

FROM LOFTY HEIGHTS

This is the story of my life. It is my hope that by writing it down, others may be spared and make wiser choices than I did. My mother died when I was born; and my father, the drunkard, rued the day I was born. My grandmother raised me from my infancy until I was a child. Her love alone sustained me.

With her passing, my life was thrown into turmoil as I was forced to live with a father I scarcely knew. Living with my father, there were times when food was scarce. I remember nights when I went to bed without a bite to eat all too well when the wolves of hunger ravaged my body and my mind cried out for want.

I was a clever and eager-to-please child, all too willing to become the understudy of a much older and wiser man. He was able to teach me clever ways to quiet the hunger in my belly. My boyish smile and angelic face became my ticket to much of the merchandise that was found in the marketplace.

Being a quick study, I found the speed of my hands was often missed by the eyes of the shopkeepers. As my skills as a petty thief became more refined, I found it easier and easier to acquire anything that I desired. Days in the marketplace were always productive.

As the years of my childhood faded away and the days of my adolescence began, it became harder to acquire the things that I needed. No longer did my boyish smile and quick hands deceive the shopkeepers. Their eyes were ever watchful of my every move.

It did not take long before I fell in with other young men who were as clever as myself. We worked in pairs: one man would attract the attention of the shopkeeper while the other took from the shop that which was required for the day's meal. As our confidence in one another's abilities gradually grew, we plotted and planned more lucrative crimes: robberies that not only filled our bellies but filled our pockets with coins as well.

We were very selective in choosing our targets. We looked for merchants with large purses, and we were all too willing to lighten their load. Most of the time, our intended victims did not even realize that they had been robbed, and by the time that the robbery was discovered, my partner and I were gone from the scene of the crime.

During one of our days in the marketplace, we were distracted from our own pursuits by a major disturbance in the temple area. Our investigation revealed that there was an angry young man in the temple making quite a fuss. He was turning over the tables of the money changers and chasing the temple merchants out of the temple with a whip made of rope.

My partner and I knew that the Roman guards would soon arrive to put down this disturbance. The Roman guards soon arrived, and seeing that the disturbance was in the temple grounds left, they did not want to become entangled in problems that concerned the Jews. After the crowed had dispersed and things settled down, I asked one of the onlookers who the young man was. He told me that He was a teacher, and He claimed that the money changers were defiling His father's house.

Sometime after this first chance meeting, I became somewhat curious and wanted to know more about this teacher.

One day, I had the opportunity to go and listen to what this young teacher had to say. I and many others followed Him to this mount where He climbed up so that the whole crowed could see him and began to teach the people. He spoke to us with such authority that I could not help but listen to what He was saying.

His words seemed to be spoken not to a crowd but to each individual person. He started His teaching with "blessed are the poor in spirit, for theirs is the kingdom of God." As He continued with His teaching, my mind went back to a happier time, when my grandmother cradled me in her arms and told me how much she loved me.

At the end of His teaching, my mind was filled with confusion. My heart and my head were in two different places.

During my twenty-five years as a thief, I have never once thought of how my actions have affected the victims of my crimes. I only know that my life as a thief has filled my belly with the finest food and drink that money can buy, and the coins in my purse have allowed me to fall asleep in the arms of young and beautiful women.

I'm not a foolish man. I know that the laws of Rome deal harshly with thieves. It is with this knowledge about the law that my partner and I carefully planned each step of a robbery before we make any kind of a move on a prospective mark. For several weeks, we have been working on one last big score. Everything must be just right: the right place, the right time of day, and the shopkeeper with the most money. This time, we are not going to steal just the shopkeeper's purse. This time, we want to steal his treasure chest. We know that robbing a house has more risk than taking a purse.

Tonight is the night. The locked door to the merchant's house presented no problem for us, and we causally and stealthily slip into the house. We move quietly through the large plush front of the house. Every step brings us closer to our prize.

The merchant's money chest is in a closet on the west wall of his bedroom. Our watching and planning have served us well thus far. The merchant is a sound sleeper, and we move slowly and carefully through his bedroom to the closet. The money is within our reach when suddenly to our surprise, guards move out of the shadows and apprehend us.

In the morning, we are handed over to Roman guards. They bind us in chains and take us before the Roman procurator, Pontius Pilate. He quickly decides our punishment. Following Roman law, we are to be crucified for our crimes. While we await our punishment from the bared window of my jail cell, I see that the young teacher is being put to the lash. I wonder what Roman law He has broken. From the way He spoke on the mount that day, I know that He could not be a common criminal due to the many kind words spoken that day.

It is early morning when the Roman guards come to my cell and get me to walk that long journey to the place where I am to be crucified. All night, I have thought about the many crimes that I have committed, and my heart is heavy with grief.

As I walk along the road, I can hear the crowd cheering and shouting at the young teacher as He is forced to carry His cross to Golgotha. My partner and I are crucified along with the young teacher, one on His left and one on His right. All morning long, the same people that He once taught swear and mock Him. They call Him king of the Jews.

As I feel my life slowly melt away and before it is too late, I ask the young teacher to remember my name. It is Achar, and I request that He remember me when He comes into His kingdom.

AT THE FOOT OF THE CROSS

The Roman legion has been my home and my life for the past ten years. My name is Claudias, and I am a soldier of Rome, a soldier worth my salt. Like many soldiers, I love my country and have pledged my alliance to my emperor.

In the name of Rome, I have fought in many campaigns. On the battlefield, there are many things that happen that one wishes to forget. At night, when the mind is quiet and the soul is awakened, this is the time when the nightmares of battle are stirred up. With the first flush of the morning sun, the nightmares evaporate with the dawn, and a new day in the life of a Roman soldier begins.

Today, we received orders for the legion to march to the city of Jerusalem. I remember all too well the first time the mighty army of Rome marched on the city of Jerusalem. The city was well fortified, and the battle that ensued was long and difficult. Many of my comrades fell at my side, and countless Jews were slain in the battle. In the end, the might of Rome prevailed.

This time, we march to calm the fears of Pontius Pilate. I have heard talk among the men. It seems that a young teacher has been arrested. His followers call him Messiah, these Jews and their Messiah. Pilate worries over nothing. The soldiers I march with are the best trained, best equipped, and seasoned soldiers in the Roman army.

After a two-day march, we are finally at the gates of the city. Some of the men are to garrison outside of the city gates, and some are to garrison in the palace yard. Six of us are assigned to guard the prisoner. I watch and listen closely as chief priest and Pharisees question the young teacher. Their questions are cleverly laid out, like a cat toying with a mouse. The teacher whose name is Jesus answers their questions clearly and honestly, knowing full well he is walking into their thinly disguised trap.

The chief priests and Pharisees, afraid of a revolt by the people who follow Jesus, send him to Pilate to be judged. I and five other soldiers accompany the young man Jesus to the Praetorium. When Pilate makes his appearance, I note that he is a thin, pale-skinned, and nervous man. Pilate questions Jesus to see if he has broken any Roman laws. Jesus is a Jew and not a Roman citizen. He must obey Roman laws but is not protected under Roman law. To the vengeful anger of the chief priests and the Pharisees, Pilate orders that Jesus be scourged.

I have men sent before the lash. I have seen the fear in their eyes. As I look into the eyes of this man Jesus, I do not see fear. Some would say the He goes like a lamb to the slaughter, but I assure you this is not the case. I have seen bravery in battle, and this man went with determination and purpose to what lay before him.

I and the other soldiers accompany Jesus to the pillory where the scourging is to take place. The sergeant at arms is a muscular and robust man. He is a skilled technician with the Roman scourge and the *flagrum*. He has carried out this assignment countless times on Roman soldiers who disobeyed orders and criminals who have broken the laws of Rome. The sergeant delivers each blow of the scourge with accuracy and precision. Standing at attention and looking on, I cannot help but count each strike of the scourge as I have done many times as I watch this punishment being carried out.

Thirty-seven, thirty-eight, thirty-nine—I take a deep breath. That's it. That's the most that can be delivered by law. The sergeant continues the scourging. I am at first startled, and then I realize that this young man is not a Roman citizen. It seems as if an eternity of time has passed when the sergeant finally stops. He is exhausted and covered in sweat and splatters of blood.

I force myself to look at the wreck of a man that is hanging from the pillar. Pilate's personal bodyguards come out and cut Jesus down from the pillar. I breathe a momentary sigh of relief as I believe that the sentence has been carried out. I stand in amazement, embarrassment, and shame as I watch the guards place a crown of thorns upon the young man's head, then pound on the crown, punch his face, and pluck at his beard.

I am a soldier. I do not take any pleasure in torturing my enemies. Slowly, I realize that these guards not only wish to embarrass the Jews. They hate the Jews and want to make an example out of this young Jewish man.

I walk the Via Dolorosa with Jesus as he carries his cross to Golgotha. With each step, he struggles beneath the weight of the cross. I cannot help but wonder what kind of a man this is. Where does his inner strength come from? If Rome only had soldiers made of this inner strength, there is no army, no land that Rome could not conquer.

As I stand at the foot of this cross, some emotion inside of me is stirred. I would be honored to fight at this man's side, for I have witnessed great bravery. I look upon this man Jesus, and I cannot help but wonder in my disciplined mind why a man would undergo these atrocities for a soldier like me.

I have killed and looted, all in the name of Rome. As if this man Jesus can read my very thoughts, our eyes meet, and with His arms stretched out on the cross, He answers me, "Because I love you this much."

A WEAVER'S JOURNEY

Jacob and Ruth anxiously awaited the birth of their first child. The two young lovers had grown up together as children in the small town of Magdalena. Like all new parents, their excitement for this first child filled their minds with wonder. After many months of waiting, the day for Ruth to give birth finally arrived. As the couple gazed at their firstborn child, a beautiful baby girl, all their fears and worries were laid to rest. The couple had decided to name their baby girl after Ruth's mother. Her name would be Mary.

Days after the birth of his daughter, Jacob had to return to his tailor shop. He had many orders to complete before the week's end. He was one of the finest tailors in the town, and his wife, Ruth, was the most skilled weaver in the region. Together, the couple fashioned the most beautiful garments in the area. Customers came from nearby towns and villages to purchase their clothing. The designs and quality of Ruth's weaving was greatly sought after. Customers often waited weeks for Ruth to complete their orders.

As their young daughter grew, she became quite skilled at weaving, designing, and tailoring fine cloths.

When Mary was just eighteen years old, both of her parents were taken from her by an epidemic that swept through their town. Many of the older inhabitants of the town were either dead or dying. After the death of her mother and father, Mary tried in vain to live in the town she called home. Even with all her skills, she did not have the same reputation as her parents. Most of the work that she did acquire was only small mending and repair jobs.

She was grateful for the work she did get, but the small payment she did receive for her services was just enough to purchase meager portions of food. After several weeks of struggle and hunger, Mary realized that the town she loved was very small and had few inhabitants left for her to survive. With her heart heavy with sorrow, she packed up her few belongings.

She thought about how she would miss the town of her childhood as she traveled the long dusty road to the city. With each step toward her new life, the sorrow within her lessened. When at last she could see the city in the distance, a glimmer of hope began to grow in her soul, and her spirit was lifted.

As Mary entered the city gates of Jerusalem, she was overwhelmed by the number of people in the streets. People were rushing here and there, buying what they needed from all the merchants. Her first thought was to find lodging for the night and rest her weary feet from the long and difficult journey.

She awoke early the next morning to the pains of hunger. In her haste to find lodging, she had forgotten to buy something to eat. As Mary greeted the new day, she observed that even at this early hour, people were still scurrying about. She found a booth where she bought dried dates and a small bit of flat bread for her breakfast.

As soon as she finished her breakfast, she went about setting up a booth in the city center with the other merchants. She put on display her finest weaving and tailored clothing. Day after day, she set up her booth, hoping she would get some customers. Each day, she watched her living expenses diminish. With fewer funds to spend, her allotment for food became smaller. With each passing day, the pain of hunger got louder and louder, like a lion that roars out impending doom.

As the sun set, Mary watched as a rich merchant slowly devoured his meal of poultry, figs, flat bread, honeycombs, and wine. The merchant saw Mary looking at his meal. With lust in his heart and with his sense of morality dulled by the wine, he invited her to join in his banquet. The gnawing pain of hunger in her belly was far greater than her embarrassment and shame.

As she ate, the merchant ordered more wine. With each glass of wine, Mary's inhibitions slipped away. The next morning, as the cobwebs cleared from her head, Mary found herself in bed with the merchant. She had never been in bed with a man before. When the merchant awoke, he gave her more money than she had seen in weeks. She got up and quickly dressed and left the room. Returning to her booth in the city center, she hoped that today, customers would come seeking a tailor or someone skilled at weaving.

Customers did come, but they were not seeking a tailor or weaver. It was on this day that she discovered that gossip could destroy a woman's reputation as quickly as a fire aided by the wind moves over an open field. With her reputation ruined, a lifestyle that she did not choose started to unfold before her very eyes.

Many of the self-righteous men from the Sanhedrin came seeking their self-pleasures with her. It was one of these very men that accused her of fornication and adultery. She was dragged out into the street to be stoned. Mary did not comprehend all that was being said. She only heard the loud voices of men arguing and shouting.

Then in the next moment, there was only silence. A young man was helping her to her feet. He told her to go on her way and be not enslaved to the sins of men. Mary gazed into His eyes and saw only tenderness and compassion. With his words of forgiveness and love, he mended the tattered fabric of her life.

The next day, she followed the man named Jesus at a distance. She heard only words of love and caring about a God who sounded more like a loving father, not the wrathful and punishing God that the Sanhedrin taught. She followed the young rabbi for several days. Listening to the young teacher was not difficult. He not only preached charity and respect for his fellow men; he lived it each day.

Mary knew that a man who said and did the right thing in spite of the criticism of others was a rare man indeed. When the Pharisees and Sadducees came accusing Jesus of blasphemy, Mary knew how quickly gossip and false words could destroy a person's reputation. She wished she could restore his dignity as he once did hers.

She stood in the courtyard with the crowd as they condemned him to death. She followed him to Calvary and wept bitter tears as she saw him hang upon a cross. After his body was taken down from the cross, Mary, along with other women, helped to prepare his body for burial.

All that were gathered watched mournfully as they laid this man Jesus in a borrowed tomb. Mary returned to the tomb after the Sabbath to say her final goodbyes. When she found the stone rolled back and the tomb opened, she rushed in and found a young man dressed in brilliant white clothing. He told her that the Jesus she was looking for had risen.

With these words, her heart skipped a beat, for she knew that the words that Jesus had spoken had been fulfilled. She found the burial shroud neatly folded where his body was once laid. She picked it up and held it to her heart, a parting gift from a beloved friend.

EMMAUS

People with sight often fail to see magic before their very eyes. I'm not talking about the magic that you see on a stage. The kind of magic I'm talking about is all around us. It's the dew in the morning that kisses each blade of grass. It's the gentle breeze that washes over clear blue waters, and it's the sound of ocean waves as they gently brush the shore.

All these wonders I have never seen, for I was born blind. I know these things because I listen to travelers as they walk and talk along the road to Emmaus. Their conversations often end abruptly when I'm spotted.

I have sat along this same stretch of road for most of my life, begging for a few coins from generous travelers. Many who pass along this road often call me Emmaus, for I can be found in the same spot day after day. An old woman named Anna has befriended me, and for several years now, she has brought me food. She takes from my basket the few coins that I have collected and prepares my meals.

Most of the time, there is only enough money to buy old stale bread and a small dried date. No matter what Anna brings, I'm thankful to her and I praise God for His generosity. Caravans of camels pass by me each and every day. The merchants from these caravans are usually very generous, and most will give me two of three coins from their purse. I thank them and tell them that I will offer prayers on their behalf.

With the dawn of each new day, I know that I have much to be thankful for. Although my eyes are closed to the outside world, my other senses have been heightened. I can smell fresh bread being baked in the nearby village. I can hear the sweet sound of a nearby cricket as he calls for his mate. I can feel moisture in the air before the rain starts to fall, and my sense of taste tells my foolish belly what will calm its foolish grumbling.

Of all my senses, I am most thankful for my sense of hearing, for it is this sense that allowed me to hear two men as they walked along the road to Emmaus. Hearing their words changed my lot in life. As I listened in on their conversation, I heard them talking about a young teacher that they had been following.

There was excitement in their voices when they spoke about the many wondrous healings that they had witnessed, and there was sadness in their voices as they talked about how their teacher was hung upon a cross. I could hear the fear in the tone of their voices as they talked about what might be their own fate. They feared that they might be hunted down and suffer the same fate as their teacher at the hands of the Roman soldiers.

Their conversation changed when I heard a third voice join them. He asked what they were discussing. They asked him if he was the only one that did not know what had happened in Jerusalem, and they told him how their teacher had been betrayed by the people He loved and how He had been condemned to death.

As I listened to the voice of this new traveler, something within my spirit was stirred and I felt that my life could be changed if I but cried out for help. I'm not sure why; but in a loud clear voice, I cried out, "Master, have mercy on me."

In the moment, I sensed that He was standing in front of me, and He asked me what it was that I wanted. I answered Him, "That I might see thee with my own eyes." With His question answered, He spoke words to me that penetrated my very soul. He touched my eyes, and for the first time, the light of day filled my eyes and I have seen my master's face.

ABOUT THE AUTHOR

Joseph Nesi is a husband, father, and grandfather who would often dream of the Bible stories we know and love from a unique perspective. His late wife, Linda, insisted he put his stories to page to pass on to their grandchildren.

Joseph's talent for storytelling has entertained and touched the hearts of family and friends for many years. At their encouragement, this book, *Know Greater Love*, came to be.

A humble man, Joseph serves his bountiful Utah community, feeding widows and volunteering at the Veterans Hospital weekly. He serves as eucharistic minister and exemplifies the core values of integrity, professionalism, excellence, and respect as a member of the Knights of Columbus.

CPSIA information can be obtained
at www.ICGtesting.com
Printed in the USA
BVHW061055110123
655995BV00019BB/1246

9 781685 265656